FEB 15

This Book Belongs to - -

Farm Girl Book Series

Courtnee -- *A Farm Girl*
Sandy -- *A City Girl*
Abe -- *A Farm Boy*
Apple Acres -- *The Farm*

APPLE ACRES

The Farm

B. Kjellberg

2006

APPLE ACRES -- *The Farm*
Farm Girl Series, Book 4
Copyright © **2006**   By B. Kjellberg

Published by

Kjellberg Publishers P.O.Box 725   Wheaton, IL 60187
Printed in U.S.A.

Library of Congress Cataloging-in-Publication Data

Kjellberg, B., 1936-
    Apple Acres : the farm / B.Kjellberg
      p. cm. -- (Farm girl series ; bk.4)
    Summary: Courtnee and Abe become engaged, plan their lives
together, get married, and move into their new farm, closely
following the Amish precepts by which they were raised.
      ISBN-13: 978-0-912868-10-3
      ISBN-10:   0-912868-10-4
    1. Amish--Juvenile fiction.   [1. Amish--Fiction. 2. Farm Life
--Indiana--Fiction. 3. Christian life--fiction. 4. Indiana -- History--
--20th century--Fiction.]   I. Title.
    PZ7.K676Ap 2006
    [Fic]--dc22

2006028871

AUTHOR'S STATEMENT

It is the author's purpose in this series of books to promote devoted Christian living and Bible based moral principles. He would be pleased if everyone who reads this story would come to believe in Jesus Christ as his/her own personal Savior, or to have his/her committal to Jesus deepened.

Courtnee and her friends are portrayed as taking their vows in the Beachy Amish Church. The author has used this branch of the Amish Church because of their readiness to accept the truth of salvation in the finished work of Christ. They still cling to some of their old ways, which are not necessarily against Scripture. They provide the author a background to present a visible Christian lifestyle. He does not favor or endorse the Beachy Amish Church above any others. As believers we are not asked to isolate ourselves, but as Jesus says to His Father, "I pray not that Thou shouldest take them out of the world, but that Thou shouldest keep them from evil." John 17:15.

If the visible part of our life is merely a tradition, then we can easily be empty inside. The test in all of this is whether what is seen on the outside — our dress and life — is truly a mirror of what is on the inside.

COURTNEE AND HER FRIENDS

JACOB and MARY EMILY YODER

John Jacob (JJ)	24
Abraham	20
COURTNEE	19
Joshua	15
Evangeline	13
Samuel	10

Grandma BIELER (Mary Emily's mother)

MENNO and ANNA MAE HOSTETLER

Boaz and Sarah (married)	
James (married to Lisa Miller)	
Mary Marie	25
Jacob	22
Amy Sue	20
TEENA	18

(Courtnee's best friend)

MATTHEW and REBECCA MAC DONALD

JOHN	19
Mary Elizabeth	15
Martha (died at 3 mo.)	—
Marvin	10

ERVIN and ABIGAIL YODER

(Courtnee's Uncle and Aunt)

Maria	26
Isaac	24
Abel	22
Paul	14
Esther	12

SIMEON and ESTHER LUTZ (The school teacher)
    Carol Anne   10
    Jane   7

Nappanee Church District

EDGAR and MILDRED MILLER (Preacher)
    Lisa (Married James Hostetler)
    Peter   25
    Rachel   23
    Michael   18

City of Goshen

HENRY and ROBERTA SCHROEDER
    SANDY (Sandra)   18
        (only child)

Brushy Prairie Church District

EMIL and GERTRUDE SCHROCK
    ABRAHAM (ABE)   19
    Grace   17
    Daniel   15
    Allen (twin)   12
    Anja (twin)   12
    Cornelia (downs syndrome) 10
    Peter   6
    Jean Anne   3

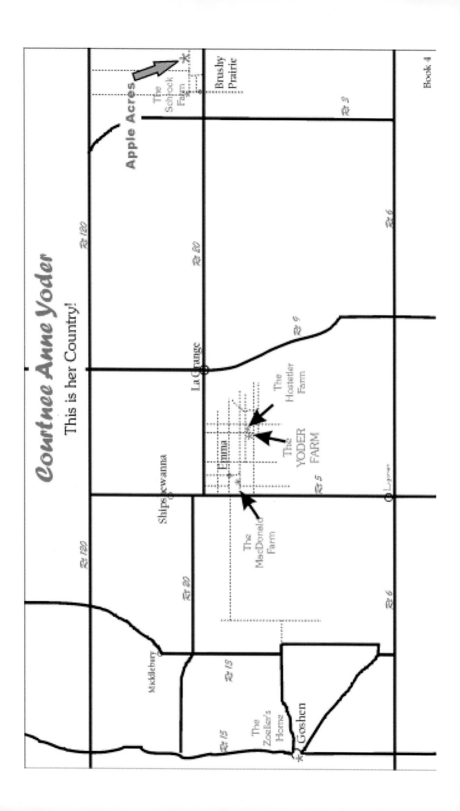

INTRODUCTION

Courtnee could not remember when she first met Teena. They had grown up being friends, as close as sisters, ever since their Papas had bought farms across the road from each other before they were born. Now with Sandy it was a different story. She had literally got blown into the Yoder farm when she and her parents were stranded in a snowstorm.

Abe's cousin brought him to a singing at the MacDonald's farm and Courtnee certainly wanted to get to know him better. John MacDonald just could not keep his eyes off the new Englisch girl who was visiting. But poor Teena, she had gone out with a guy who did not mean what he said, but she believed him.

And there she was sitting around dreaming of a guy who was running with any and every girl, while Courtnee and Sandy were building lasting friendships.

Abe's parents host a singing the first one in Brushy Prairie. Teena accepts Courtnee's invitation to attend with she and Abe, and... I can't tell you any more!

APPLE ACRES

Chapter 1

"Wow! What a singing." Courtnee said as she bounded into the seat next to Abe in his pick-up truck. "For a first one, I think that was wonderful good."

"It sure was. I was worried some of those rowdy kids would come — I know they knew about it. In fact one of them came up to me at the gas station and asked if it was true that we were having a singing. I just looked him square in the eye and replied slowly that 'yes, we were.' I didn't want him to feel invited, because he never attends meeting anyway."

"I loved some of those new tunes that Simeon started. I think it's kinda' nice to learn new ones. None of us are very good singers. We need to practice."

"I don't know where Simeon learned those. He may have learned them out in Ohio — they moved here just about the time Everett was born." Abe thought Courtnee would take the "bait" when he used Everett's name, and it worked.

"Isn't it nice that Everett took Teena home. I sure hope she can now forget Michael Miller. Everett doesn't seem like Mike's kind as far as I can tell. He seems more sober and sensible. Is he?"

"He is. We've always been good friends. He's definitely not a rounder. He's a good farmer too. I think in some ways better than his father."

"Well, I sure hope he and Teena get on well — I guess they had never met before tonight. I sure hope it works out. Teena and I have been so close all our lives that I really want to see her happy again. You know, nearly her whole depression about Mike was because of going with him only once and a passionate kiss. It was all in her head. I think she didn't join church with me just because of her fantasy about Mike. Well, I hope she learned to take it to the Lord."

"Everett is definitely not Mike's type. He's much different."

After Abe spoke neither of them spoke for a while. It was very dark and they could see nothing but the road in the headlights. But Courtnee was remembering her long conversations with Teena, and how she had convinced Teena to attend this singing with she and Abe. She was so glad it turned out this way, and the sparkle in Teena's eyes told her she was excited too.

As they turned into the Yoder's driveway Abe said, "I think I'll see if Everett wants to go deer hunting with me. We hunt in the woods on the back of our place. We've been having a lot of trouble with deer lately and besides the season just opened. Do you like venison?"

"It depends… sometimes it's tough and stringy. It makes good sausage though. My Papa has a gun, but he seldom goes hunting with it. Do you have a gun?"

"Yes, I have a twelve gauge shotgun. However, for deer Everett and I use bow and arrow."

"Bow and arrow? I thought only Indians used those!" exclaimed Courtnee, "Why do you use bow and arrow?"

"I feel it gives the deer more of a chance, and it's sort of a challenge to stalk the prey. Everett is really good with the bow. Last year each of us got a deer. They are corn-fed deer, because they have been eating out of our field, which makes them taste really good. Would your parents like some of the meat if we get one?"

"Oh, sure! They are game for anything – sorry for the pun."

"Oh, yeah… game!" Abe said as he began to laugh, "You caught me on that one."

As Courtnee opened the truck door she said, "Thanks for another wonderful evening."

"Oh! Here I'll walk you to the door," he said as he ran around the truck to help her out. As they walked to the door, hand in hand, he said, "There's something about being with you... don't ever change."

"Thanks, Abe," was all she could say.

*****

On Friday of that week as Courtnee was cleaning up the lunch dishes her mother announced, "Courtnee you have a visitor! He just drove in."

"Oh, good!" She exclaimed as she ran to open the door.

There was a light dusting of snow on the ground. It was very cold and as Abe came up the path his breath looked like he was smoking and Courtnee began to laugh. "You look like a forest fire coming up the path."

"Well, forest fire or not, I brought you some venison. Everett and I each got a nice young buck. One arrow each was all it took!" And he dumped his armload of packages on the table. "I dropped Everett at Teena's just now — he also took them some of his buck."

"Oh, hey, I've got an idea! What if we had Everett and Teena come over here for the afternoon and then we could have venison for supper — that would be fun. We could play some games or something."

"That would be fine, but you'll need to get clearance from someone else, won't you?" Just then Courtnee's mother entered the room and he said, "I brought you a present, Mary Emily."

"Well, what have we got here? Shall I open one?"

"No, you really don't need to, it's some of the buck I shot on Wednesday."

"Oh, how nice of you. We'll have to have a feast." Just the words Courtnee wanted to hear her mother say.

"Mamma, I was wondering if we could have Everett and Teena over this afternoon and stay for supper? We could play some games in here since it is too cold to go out."

"Well, actually... wait a minute, you said Everett? He lives pretty far away for this afternoon."

"I always get ahead of myself. Abe dropped Everett at Teena's before coming here. Everett shared some of his buck with them, too."

"Oh, I see! Sure that would be just fine. I'll do some mending and sewing this afternoon, and then we'll have venison for supper and they can stay. Why don't you and Abe drive over there and see if they want to come?"

It did not take Courtnee long to get her coat on and they were off, but she forgot that Abe's pick-up truck had only one seat so they had to pack in for the short ride back. There was a lot of giggling and laughing, so much so that they steamed up the windows of the truck and Abe could hardly see to drive.

Courtnee was really pleased to get acquainted with Everett, because she cared deeply for her friend Teena and was really hoping Teena had found the right beau. He was not at all like Teena's father. Her father loved to laugh and told lots of jokes, but Everett was more serious. He got along very well with Sam and Evangeline — they loved him. *Always a good test of a future husband is how he gets along with children,* Courtnee thought, remembering how her brothers and sister loved Abe.

Both Abe and Everett had to recount their hunting expedition for Joshua and Sam. They told about seeing a buck with a huge set of antlers but not being able to get a shot at him. Bow hunting requires the ability to walk almost without making a sound, as well as to keep track of the direction of the wind because deer have very good noses. Josh and Sam were drinking all of this in. Soon Sam was practicing walking without making a sound, which was pretty hard for him.

When the story got to the butchering of the dead deer the girls did not want to hear so they went out to the kitchen. Oh well, it was about time to start supper anyway. They had to get some advice from Mary Emily about cooking the venison and even Abe and Everett had some suggestions to make. One of Grandma Beiler's recipes came in handy.

Chapter 2

The dinner was a success and Abe, and Everett and Teena were finally on the way home. *What a wonderful afternoon as well as supper feasting on venison,* Courtnee thought.

She had hardly finished thinking this when Abraham came bursting into the house announcing that Papa had fallen and he thought he had a broken leg. There was a scurry of coats and scarves being hastily put on as everyone wanted to be the first to reach their father. He was moaning in great pain as Mary Emily tried to determine what the problem was. He dared not move or he would cry out in pain.

"Evangeline, would you run quickly to Hostetler's and see if Menno could come and help. Courtnee get some blankets. Abraham would you lift Papa's head so I can put this under to make him more comfortable?"

To Mary Emily it seemed that it took Courtnee an hour to get the blankets when it actually was only several minutes. "Whatever happened, honey? Do you remember how you did this?"

"No," Jacob mumbled, "all of a sudden I was on the floor and my leg was hurting something awful."

"Are you sure it is only your leg? What about your back, is it OK?"

"Yeah, I'm sure it's my leg. Abraham had better see to the milking tonight."

"That's why I wanted Menno to come and go to the hospital with us, he also can help get you in the car. Abraham, you can do Pappa's chores," she said, as she tucked the blankets around him. He was already shivering quite badly from the cold and shock.

"Jacob is this another one of your tricks?" Said Menno as he walked up.

"I wish that's all it was, but I'm afraid it's worse than that. Would you mind driving Mary Emily and I to the hospital?" Jacob's teeth chattered as he talked because of shivering.

It was no easy task getting Jacob into Menno's car, and it caused him considerable pain. Finally, the job was done and Menno and Mary Emily were on their way to the hospital with Jacob half sitting and half laying in the back seat. Courtnee, Abraham, Joshua, Evangeline, and Sam all headed for the house as quickly as they could. They were all frozen and a bit scared not knowing what to expect. Each was quiet as they wondered what this would mean for their family. With Papa unable to work — who would do his work? Of course, Abraham was certainly capable and willing, but he could not do it all. Courtnee used to help milk the cows, *but* she reasoned, *Joshua could do that now that he is old enough.* She could not picture her father just sitting around. He was always working — this would be a big change for him, at least until his leg healed.

As the evening wore on she found herself wondering what was going on at the hospital. Would they have to operate, or just put it in a cast? She tried to sew, but that did not work. She tried to read, but her thoughts kept going back to the hospital. She remembered the time Joshua broke his arm and how long it was before her parents and Joshua came home. But that time Abe had come and stayed for supper, which made the evening much more pleasant. *Well,* she told herself, *you can't complain, Courtnee, you had a really fun afternoon and supper hour this very day.*

She let her thoughts run back to the afternoon and dinner with her friends. As she got to know Everett she found she liked him more and more — she was so pleased that Teena now had a very good boy friend. They seemed to get along so well and were at ease with each other, which she thought was a good sign. *Everett is nice, but I won't trade Abe for Everett, no thank you!* she said to herself.

"Courtnee," Evangeline said as she looked up from the book she was reading, "are you going to marry Abe?"

The question took her by surprise. "Why do you ask?"

"Well, I was just wondering what it would be like around here when you and Abraham are both married and it's just Josh and Sam and me. Will Papa be able to walk, do you think?"

"I have no idea, but I would guess he won't be able to until his leg heals anyway."

"If he can't work who is going to do all his work?" Eve's mind was obviously running in the same groove that Courtnee's was.

"Well, I suppose Josh could do the milking, or at least some of it. Sam can help do the feeding. Papa will have to tell them what to do, but I think they could do it."

As Courtnee spoke Josh looked up from *The Plain News* newspaper that he had been reading, "What did you say I could do?"

"I said I thought you could help with the milking while Papa is recovering — you know how to milk."

"But I've already got other jobs to do."

"I know, but we are all going to have to work a little harder so that all the work still gets done."

"Now you sound like Mamma!" And he went back to his newspaper.

The evening went by slowly for Courtnee. Abraham and Joshua went to bed because they knew they would be expected to perform their father's duties in the morning, which meant getting up very early. Then she sent Sam and Evangeline to bed so they could be ready for school, but she waited up hoping her parents and Menno would be home soon. Her eyes kept wanting to go to sleep, but her mind kept saying, *stay awake!* But when the back door bumped open at midnight she was startled awake, and she never did know how long she slept.

"Well, are you still up?" Her father said as he clumped into the kitchen on his crutches.

"Wanted to see you when you came home, hoping you weren't too bad hurt. What was it?"

"My knee was partly dislocated and several torn ligaments. The doctor said I can't walk on it for about six weeks. All I need... to just sit around all winter!"

"Well, you always tell us kids that the Lord knows best," Courtnee smiled at him and then gave him a kiss on his whiskery face.

"You're right, sweetie. I should just accept it from Him, but it's going to be hard." Jacob said as he half sat and half fell into his favorite chair.

"Well, I'll be going Jacob — nothing else I can do for you?" Menno said as he stood in the living room doorway.

"Nothing at all. Thanks many times over for all you did. I am sorry to have kept you out so late, but we could not have done it ourselves. Greet Anna Mae for us."

"OK, bye then!"

After a cup of hot chocolate, Courtnee and her mother helped Jacob out of the chair and onto his crutches, which he was very clumsy with as yet. They all went to bed hoping to get some sleep before the alarm went off in the early morning darkness.

*****

Abraham and Joshua kept the farm running, and quite smoothly at that, but they had to work very hard. It was about three weeks before the weather was good enough for Jacob to hop out to the barn on his crutches to "check on things." But he found that he was a long way from doing anything without the crutches, and even the old horse *Blaze* shied away from him when she saw his crutches. However, he was amazed how well the boys were coping. Everything was where it should be and the stalls were clean as well. "You boys have done an excellent job. You will never know how much I appreciate this."

"Thanks, Papa!" they both said at once.

The weeks were very long, but after reading everything he could find he then started in to sewing. His mother had made him sew when he was young. After the first little bit of childish rebellion he had begun to enjoy sewing. So one day Mary Emily went along with the Hostetlers to Shipshewanna and she bought him several cross-stitch projects. He enjoyed it, *At least it is something to do*, he thought.

It was nearly eight weeks before he could walk without the crutches, and by then he was quite wobbly. His leg muscles had become weak from just sitting. He had to walk a lot to gain strength. But gradually his strength returned and he was able to begin doing more of the work.

Chapter 3

One day Abe arrived when Courtnee was not expecting him. It was mid-morning and he said he had to get some feed from the mill. He wanted Courtnee to go along. "We'll be back about mid-afternoon, will that be alright?" He asked.

"I'll check with Mamma, but I think it's OK."

He had not been to the mill yet so they headed there and got what he needed, actually it was a supplement he wanted to try on his herd. It was lunchtime by the time he loaded his purchases into the truck so they headed over to the café. For Courtnee it was a treat to eat at the café because she seldom got to go there.

After lunch he turned the car toward Brushy Prairie and then down a gravel road, which she did not recognize. They never seemed to run out of things to talk about and today was no exception. So much so that she had not even noticed that Abe was slowing the car, but when he turned out into a hay field she was startled.

"What are you doing? This is a field... are you..."

"Don't worry, this is our field."

"I thought you were taking me home. What's the deal?"

As Abe turned the car around to face the road he said, "I have something to ask you and I don't want anyone else to hear." Then he realized how ridiculous what he just said sounded like, and he started to laugh, but it was a nervous laugh.

She laughed too, as she asked, "You mean if we are on the road someone else might hear?" However, her laugh was a nervous one too, because this seemed really out of the ordinary. She did not know what to expect.

"No, I mean… what do I mean? Anyway, I wanted to concentrate on the question and not on driving." Abe was nervous although he thought he had this all planned out.

Oh, dear, Courtnee thought, *what is coming? Lord help me to answer right.* "What are you talking about?" She questioned him softly.

"Well," he cleared his throat for the umpteenth time, "Well, I… I don't know any other way to say this… you know we've been seeing each other a lot, and have gotten to be best friends… and what's happened is I have fallen in love with you and… well, would you consider getting married?" Only then did he turn to look at her.

Yes, this is it! Well, Courtnee, give him an answer! Don't pretend you didn't know it was coming — you did! Courtnee's mind was spinning.

"You mean marry *you*?" Then suddenly it hit her *He really means it!* She felt like she was tongue-tied, and could not think what to say.

"I wouldn't ask you to marry anyone else, would I?" His laugh was more nervous now.

"Yes, Abe... yes I will!" She finally squeaked out, and then in a soft voice, "I love you…" and then she choked up and could not say any more as tears started to come to her eyes.

"Ever since the first day we met at MacDonald's you were all I could think about. I can't tell you how much I love you." Abe reached and took her hand in his, and they sat there a long time looking at each other with smiles on their faces and tears in their eyes.

When Abe dropped her off it was almost time for supper and her father was in the house already. Jacob found that his leg got tired quicker than the rest of him,

---

Apple Snow

½ cup Sugar
1 cup Apple pulp
1 tablespoon lemon juice
3 egg whites

Beat egg whites stiff, fold in sugar, lemon juice and apple pulp. Serve cold in sherbet glasses with spoonful of soft custard over the snow. Serves 6 or 8.

---

but he did not want to risk falling again. She did not say anything at supper about her engagement, nor did she say anything that evening. She wanted to talk to her mother alone first and the time was never just right.

So Courtnee had to go to bed with her secret untold and she was about to explode, then she decided she would tell Jesus and she did just that. She asked Him for help in the days ahead, and she asked Him to help her to be a subject wife for Abe, but she never finished because she had fallen asleep.

Morning came much earlier than usual for her, and it was still dark when she bounded out of bed nearly sending Evangeline onto the floor. She had suddenly remembered that she was engaged! She could hardly believe it was finally real. Even though she had gone to bed late and even then could not sleep for a long time — now she was wide-awake. Her heart was already pounding as she combed her hair. When could she tell her mother — what should she say? Should she tell her brothers… or Evangeline? When she got to the kitchen she met her mother just coming to start her day.

"Courtnee, you are sure up early. Are you feeling all right? Your face is flushed something awful."

"No, I am alright… just woke up and couldn't sleep."

"I am worried about you because your face is so flushed. Let's get some tea going, but first I've got to start the fire. Would you bring a little firewood from the porch? I guess Abraham forgot to fill the wood box last night. I think he's got girls on his mind. Oh well, I hope some tea will settle you down."

As Courtnee came in with the firewood she could not hold her secret any longer. "Mamma, guess what!"

"Go ahead, I can't guess."

"Abe asked me to marry him!"

"What did you tell him?"

"Yes! I told him, 'Yes!' This has to be my happiest day, Mamma!"

"Oh, my dear girl! I am so pleased for you." Her mother exclaimed as she gave her a strong hug and held her tight, while Courtnee burst into tears of excitement and joy. When she could get her composure she looked up and her mother was drying her eyes. "This *is* a wonderful day, don't you ever forget it. I am so happy for you. I don't think there is a nicer guy. Ooops! There goes the tea boiling — let's have a cup."

As they had their tea they talked about all that most certainly will happen, and when a wedding day could be set. About where they would live, and would Abe be able to buy a farm of his own. Abe and Courtnee had not had time to talk about these things either, but her mother was so excited for them that her mind was spinning too. When Courtnee's father came through the kitchen to go out to do the early morning chores he saw them both sitting at the table and was surprised that Courtnee was up so early, but neither of them said a word. Her mother wanted to break the news at breakfast when everyone would be there. Getting a kitchen started in the morning with a wood fired cookstove, and to begin cooking breakfast took quite a bit of work. With her father gone to the barn they continued their discussion while they worked, but in hushed tones.

Later, when her father and Abraham came in from the barn everyone assembled around the table; then were seated, gave thanks for the food, and the chatter began. Their father began by saying what he planned to do and gave Abraham, Joshua, and Sam their jobs for the day. Mary Emily spoke about what she intended to do, and then what Courtnee and Evangeline would do. When this was finished Courtnee's father turned to her and said, "Are you alright? You look really flushed this morning."

"Jacob," Mary Emily interjected, "Courtnee has a wonderful announcement to make."

At that moment Courtnee felt as though she would faint. *This is it! Everyone will know now. I think it is wonderful, so I'll go ahead and say it.* "Well, I can't keep it a secret — Abe and I are engaged to be married!"

Her father jumped out of his chair and came around the table to her as she stood up and wrapping her in his arms said, "I am so pleased, sweetie! May the Lord bless you and keep you in His love." But in his heart he felt a pain because she was... well, sort of, his pet, and she would be leaving.

Evangeline came running over to her and threw her arms around her and began to cry, while Abraham shrugged and said, "So, big deal. Why is everyone crying?" Just then Sam put his head down on the table and she could hear a snuffle or two.

Chapter 4

That afternoon Courtnee walked over to Teena's house to tell her of the good news.

She knocked lightly on the door and walked in to hear Anna Mae say, "Come on in!"

"Hi, Anna Mae!"

"Hi Courtnee, what brings you here today?"

"Oh, just thought I'd have a visit with Teena if she's home." Courtnee tried to sound very casual.

"Teena was here a minute ago. She may have gone to collect the eggs, but she'll be back in a minute. Would you have a tea?"

"That sounds good if you have the water hot."

"The water is always hot. Think I'll have a cup with you it's about time for my mid-afternoon tea. Oh, there comes Teena now."

As Teena came in she was struggling with the basket brim full of eggs and without looking up she said, "I think that old red hen is trying to sit again, we're going to have to do something about it." Then as she looked up. "Oh!" she exclaimed when she saw Courtnee, "Surprise! What brings you here?"

"Oh, nothin' really, just thought I'd let you in on a secret."

"Secret?" Teena nearly shouted.

Courtnee could not hold it in any longer, and she burst out with, "I'm engaged!!"

Teena stood in stunned silence for a brief second and then screamed, "Wonderful!" and rushing over to Courtnee, threw her arms around her and proceeded to cry. Anna Mae had been pouring the tea when Courtnee let her secret out, and turning around joined the two girls and all three of them laughed and cried together.

"I am so happy for you, but we are going to miss you terribly."

"I don't know what I'll do without you," Teena said as she wiped her eyes, "We're as close as sisters. I am so happy for you — Abe is such a nice guy. You couldn't have done better. He's the second best guy I know!" She had to laugh as she said "second best."

"You are right I think the Lord has blest us both with two of the nicest guys around. I was really glad to get to know Everett that afternoon before Papa's accident. Actually, we may wind up being neighbors again, who knows."

"Maybe, but we have just started courting."

"Girls, let's all have our tea and we'll have a piece of apple pie to celebrate," Anna Mae said as she set three pieces of pie on the table. At that moment who should walk in but Menno.

"Well, well, what's going on? It looks like a party and I wasn't invited!"

"We didn't leave you out, Menno," Anna Mae confessed, "but Courtnee has something wonderful to tell you."

"Abe and I are engaged!" Courtnee blurted out.

"You are engaged? Wonderful! Fantastic!" he rushed over to her and engulfed her in his bear-like arms, in a tight hug. "I am so pleased for you, I am sure you will be happy." Then as he stepped back, "Now don't forget to come back once in a while and see old uncle Menno!" and gave his usual chuckle.

"Oh, don't worry, I won't be that far away." She giggled.

"May the Lord bless you and Abe and keep you near to Him always.

"You know what? I just heard a new joke! This mother said to her son, 'Johnnie, did you finish filling the salt shaker?' Johnnie said, 'Not yet! It takes a long time getting it in those little holes.'" Menno always loved jokes he told, and doubled over in laughter. When he finally recovered himself enough he said, "I love these jokes.

"Oh, here is another one; there was this girl who told a guy, who had just asked her out, 'I wouldn't go out with you in a million years!' And you know what he said? 'OK, I'll wait!'" This time Menno's face turned bright red from laughing so hard.

When they all had settled down from the jokes and Courtnee's surprise she decided it was time to head home. What a visit it had been!

*****

As Courtnee pulled the mail from the mailbox she spied a letter from Sandy. *Oh, Sandy, that's someone I haven't told about my engagement — how could I forget her?* She could not wait to get in the house and read it. She was already composing her answer in her head, but she was in for a real shock.

Dearest Courtnee,

I can't hold in my excitement any longer. John and I are going to be married! I am so excited and my folks are too. John asked me a few days ago and we agreed neither of us would say anything until I had time to write to you. So now it is going to be talked about all over the place. I cannot tell you how happy I am. I think we are going to have to live with his parents until we can afford a place of our own, or even rent something.

Sorry, I cannot take longer to write, because I am working now — just got a job at Saxmeyer's Sewing Store. I guess I have to face the real world now. We need to save as much money as we can.

Dad and Mom are both well and asked to be remembered to your Papa and Mamma.

Warmest love from your friend,

Sandy

P.S. Remember that snowstorm — that was a thousand years ago... it seems.

Tears were streaming from Courtnee's eyes and her hand was shaking by the time she finished the letter. She was thrilled! She and Sandy were even engaged together. *Yes, Sandy, I remember the snowstorm. It must have been God who did it — He must have been planning this all along. I wonder what other things He is planning for us?*

She could not wait to get to her room and reply immediately to Sandy's letter. But suddenly when she got her paper and ballpoint pen out she got writer's block — what should she say? How should she say it? She sat there a long time letting all these thoughts run through her mind. *Oh, I've got an idea!*

Dear Sandy,

I couldn't believe my eyes when I read your letter, because Abe asked me to marry him last Friday too! Have these guys been talking behind our back? Neither of them would, I know. I am sooo thrilled for you. John is one of the best guys I know, you are going to be so happy with him. When Abe asked me I must admit I was kind of tongue-tied, but I managed to squeak out a "Yes" but I really meant, "YES!"

Would it be possible for us to get together for lunch at some restaurant? Abe told me that he wants to pick me up next Saturday and take me with him to Shipshewanna. He needs some more cattle supplement. How about if we meet at the Blue Door Restaurant? Let's set a time of 11:30 to 12:00, because you will not have time to answer this. If you can be there... good, if not we'll plan another time. It would be fun to have a talk, and maybe we could make it a surprise for the guys. Just tell John you would like to go there to celebrate.

Everybody here is fine.

See you on Saturday, your loving friend,

Courtnee

Now she would have to wait for Saturday. *This is going to be a long wait!* The more she thought about it, the stronger her feeling was to make the lunch appointment a surprise for Abe. If it looked like he wanted to change plans she was going to have to convince him that she really wanted to go to the Blue Door Restaurant.

However, she soon got back into the usual routine of chores around the house. The very first thing was to begin getting ready for supper. She had taken a long time over Sandy's letter and then her reply. *Where had the afternoon gone?*

"Mamma, Sandy's engaged too!" She exclaimed as she burst into the kitchen.

"Engaged? I can't believe it. Did you know she was going to be? How could it be the same time?" Her mother was astonished.

"No! I had no idea. I just had a letter from her. I don't think she knows about Abe and I — I forgot to write her. I feel so ashamed, here she is one of my best friends and I forgot to tell her!"

They continued talking all the while they prepared supper. They talked about Sandy's engagement as well as her own, and where John and Sandy might live, and what it would mean to their own family to have

Courtnee gone. Her mother gave her some very good advice when she said, "Sweetheart, always remember that after you are married your husband is your head. You are to look to him for everything. Don't do anything without his approval, or if you know he would approve it. This sounds funny to say but it is according

Fried Apples

6 Apples
2 tbsp melted fat

Wash and core the apples. Cut into 1/8" slices across the core of the apple. Saute in melted fat, being careful not to break the slices, and cook until soft so apples still hold their shape. Sweeten to taste with cinnamon and sugar.

to Scripture. Of course, Scripture has things to say to the husband, but your part is to honor him in everything. Right now you are so much in love with him you probably can't imagine anything different. You are a girl with a very quick mind and an organizing one, which is good, but it must be kept in its right place. Sorry for the lecture, but I hope you understand."

"Oh, I do Mamma. But we have never had a disagreement and can talk about everything easily."

"Abe is a super guy and I hope you realize there are not many around like him. I feel really sure the Lord has brought you two together, but you need to think of what I have said. Do me one favor, read Ephesians chapter five, and First Corinthians chapter seven, and also the first part of chapter eleven. These are God's words about husbands and wives. It would be good for Abe to read them as well."

"Abe and I were talking the other day about these very things. We agreed we needed help about how this all will work out. He said that he thought Scripture said I should rule the house."

"Yes, it says, 'guide the house," that is another good Scripture to read — the first part of first Timothy chapter five."

"Wow, I didn't know you knew the Bible so well!"

"Well, sweetie, the Bible is God's word. Shouldn't it be important to us? I believe it gives me direction for everything I do, and so does Papa."

"Thanks, I'll read what you suggested. Oops! I hear Papa and the boys coming and I forgot to set the table." Courtnee said as she and her mother flew into action. Her mother had been working at the stove all the while they talked, but Courtnee sat at the table with her hands under her chin drinking in what her mother was saying. As she thought about it she realized that she saw in her parents exactly what her mother was saying and it strengthened her resolve to be just like them.

Chapter 5

The days before Saturday seemed to fly by because Courtnee had, beside her normal chores, much to think about. She read the Scriptures her mother had suggested several times and almost memorized them. She was anxious to share them with Abe and see what he would say.

When Saturday morning arrived Courtnee was up bright and early aiming to get her Saturday chores done early so she would be ready well before Abe arrived. When she finished the breakfast dishes she ran to her room and changed to her clean green dress and put on her white going-to-meeting apron and prayer cap. She sat down in the parlor to wait and catch her breath. *Whew!* It had been a fast morning.

She did not have long to wait before Abe arrived, but she was all ready and hopped into the truck and they were off.

"Abe, Papa gave me money to treat for lunch. I hope you don't mind that I pay. In fact, I would like to give you the money and you can do the paying." She said as she settled in beside him.

"Well! That is very nice of him, I certainly won't object."
Jacob had never done this before and Abe was
astonished.

"I have one request, if you don't mind, I would like to
eat at the Blue Door Restaurant. We always eat at the
Café and I would like to try something different, is that
OK?"

"Actually, I have never eaten there either, so it would be
fun to try. First, I'll get the cattle supplement at the feed
mill and then we'll go there. I think the timing will be
about right."

It took a little longer at the mill than Abe had expected
so it was about 11:45 when they arrived at the
restaurant. *This is going to be so much fun,* and
Courtnee's heart began to race in anticipation.

They entered the restaurant and were soon seated, *At a
table for four, to yet!* she thought. Abe hung his hat with
all the others and Courtnee wondered *how will he
know which is his.* The waitress handed them the card
that served as a menu, but Courtnee could not
concentrate. When the door opened and John and
Sandy walked in, everyone, as usual, looked up and
Abe's mouth dropped open. He could not say anything
but, "Uh! Uh!" and Courtnee finished it, "Look who's
here!" she jumped up and went to Sandy and gave her
a big hug. They were soon all seated and the chatter
began. When Abe found out that Courtnee had
"rigged" this whole thing he was delighted.

"This can be a celebration for all of us," Sandy said,
"Only Courtnee would think of such a thing!"

"I hope I didn't overstep my place, Abe, but I thought it would be so much fun."

"What a great idea, sweetheart," he said as he reached for her hand, "but I have a surprise for you. Ha! Ha! Right after lunch we are going out to look at a small farm I hope to buy."

Courtnee nearly fainted. "Wow! I never thought..." and she could say no more. She had to put her head down because her eyes were full of tears.

John broke in to relieve her excitement, "I think that is wonderful, Abe, if you can buy a place. It looks like we are going to have to live with my parents for a while, but that won't matter if it isn't too long — right, Sandy?" as he turned to Sandy and put his hand on hers.

"John, I would live even in a barn with you."

John began to laugh, "Better be careful what you say!" and they all had a good laugh.

After a pause while they gave their order, Abe said, "I still can't get over it that you guys would come all this way just for lunch." He turned to Sandy, "Did you drive to John's?"

"Yeah, Dad said I could use the car. He is busy redecorating the living room. He thinks we'll have quite a crowd at the wedding. I think he's right."

"Do you have a date set for your wedding?" Courtnee wondered.

"Well, no, not really," John said as he turned to Sandy then back to Courtnee. "We have talked about November or early December. It doesn't matter much because we won't be starting our own place right away. We want to save as much as we can, and I think by next spring we'll be able to rent, or even buy, which would be ideal. What about you guys?"

"We really haven't got down to working on a date yet. I think I have found a place we can buy — with my parents help, of course. I have some really nice pedigreed Black Angus cattle I have raised which I can sell. I'll keep my breeding stock and just sell off some steers and heifers. That's what I was planning to surprise Courtnee with - a trip to the farm I am looking to buy to see if she approves. As for a date I guess we'll have to talk about that too." Abe turned to see sheer delight in Courtnee's eyes.

Just then their meals were served and they continued with small talk between bites. They all had broasted chicken and found it "wonderful good," to use Courtnee's words. Suddenly as they were finishing up Courtnee remembered the money. She had planned to give it to Abe before the meal. So she removed it from her pocket and reached over to him below the table and nudged him with her hand. He remembered too and calmly took it without being noticed by John and Sandy.

"Well, I guess we had better hit the road," said John as he pushed his chair back, "thanks for such a wonderful time — it truly was a surprise celebration. Keep us informed about your plans, we will do the same."

Venison Stew

4 lb. Deer shoulder	8 small Whole Onions
1 cup Tomato juice	6 medium sliced Carrots
2 tbsp Horseradish	6 Stalks Celery
Salt and Pepper to taste	2 small Turnips - halved
Flour and Shortening	8 peeled Potatoes

Roll the shoulder in seasoned flour (salt and pepper to taste) and place in a hot kettle, browning it on all sides in hot shortening. Add horseradish and tomato juice. Cover and cook slowly for 3 hours, adding water to prevent burning. About 45 minutes before end of cooking time, add onions, celery, carrots, potatoes, turnips and salt. Thicken the juice with flour for tasty gravy.

"The treat was on Jacob today, so we all need to thank him. This has been a real surprise and a lot of fun." Abe said as they all stood to go. The girls had another long hug and they walked out together.

As soon as Abe and Courtnee were in the car Abe said, "I never had a clue! You pulled that off perfectly. They are so happy together. I think Sandy is the sweetest girl; John couldn't have done better. I sure hope they will be able to get a place of their own soon. I guess his father hasn't had any help from his parents so he has had to go it alone.

"Is it alright to go over and see this farm I have found? It is directly north of Brushy Prairie and not too far from my folks place. The buildings aren't much but it's got about 40 acres of land, which would be enough for cattle. what do you say?"

"Please, let's go! It sounds exciting. I can't believe that you are talking of buying a place. Most couples have to rent for a while. It sounds really interesting."

The subject of a wedding date came up and they decided that it would be best to plan it around the purchase of this farm they were going to see. Abe thought it would depend if they had to do much work on the house and buildings before they moved in. Abe had been in it once but did not look at it in that much detail. Today he had a key from the owner so they could go through.

"An old Englisch couple lived in it until they moved to a rest home and eventually died. Their son never married and he continued to live there and run the farm until he got crippled with arthritis and had to move to LaGrange. The daughter married and lives somewhere on the west coast. The house has set for 5 or 6 years with no one there so it may need some repairs. He left most of the furniture right in it — in fact, he asked me not to mess with the desk since he left a lot of his papers in it. However, he said all the furniture goes with the house."

"Wow, it sounds like a great deal!"

As they turned in the long drive they both had all kinds of thoughts running through their heads. Even in the early spring it looked beautiful.

"It looks beautiful!" Courtnee exclaimed. "Is that an apple orchard over there?"

"It sure looks like it — that's a lot of trees. It looks like the machinery shed is nearly tumbled down. That must be the chicken coop over there. (pointing) Oh yeah, there's the outhouse — he said it hadn't been used in many years. That's another thing the house is wired for electric and has an electric pump to produce running water, and an indoor toilet. What will we do about these?" Abe was thinking out loud.

"I think I'll let you decide on those things. If we kept them would they lead us away from our committals, do you think?"

"We don't want that to happen. We should ask your Papa, and mine what they think."

"I've got it!" She suddenly exclaimed, "We'll call it 'Apple Acres' — what do you think?"

"Hey, that sounds really good, but don't you think you're getting the cart before the horse? Well, here we are... let's go in and have a look."

They both jumped out of the truck like two kids in a candy store. It did look a little run down on the outside, and as they opened the back door it was evident that nothing had been done in the way of improvements in many years. But Courtnee was really pleased with everything, even most of the furniture would be a big help.

"You know, Abe, some of this furniture looks really old and I have heard of people who buy antiques. We might be able to sell what we don't need. And as for the electric I don't know if I would even know how to live having electricity running everywhere. If we have to take it out would it be very hard?"

"I don't think it would be too hard. We would have to take down those lights on the ceiling and patch over the spot. We could leave the switches and outlets where they are. Then the electric would have to be shut off at the pole out front. The plumbing will probably be the hard part."

After going through the house and memorizing where each room was they went outside to the small barn. It was not in bad shape at all, just neglected and messy, but the machinery shed was just about to tumble down. Abe pulled the door of the outhouse open and it certainly would have to be rebuilt. The door fell right off in his hands. Still they both liked the place and decided that Abe should go ahead and try to buy it. Courtnee said she thought it would be fun making it a home.

As she went to bed that night her head was spinning with all that had happened on this wonderful day. Pictures of "Apple Acres" were glowing in her mind. She was picturing it in all it's beauty — trees in bloom, black cattle on the green grass, and she and Abe sitting outside having a cool glass of iced tea. What a dream!

Chapter 6

It took Abe quite a few days and a lot of work to figure out how to buy the farm that Courtnee was already calling Apple Acres. He spoke to his father as well as several others in his church district as to what he should do about the electric and water and the inside plumbing.

Arriving at the Yoder farm he asked Courtnee to go with him to the feed mill to get several items he needed. His main purpose, however, was to speak with Courtnee's parents about the electric and plumbing as well as a date for the wedding. He wanted to be sure everyone was satisfied. Mary Emily immediately asked him to stay for supper, which he readily accepted. Then he and Courtnee were off to get the feed, saying they would be back in time for supper.

He and Courtnee discussed what he had done about financing the farm and all the details, which were not finished by any means, but at least they were begun. They discussed, also, a possible wedding date.

"Honey, I would like to see us get the farm purchase completed and have a couple of months to work on it before we are married, then we could move right in. What do you think?"

"I think that is the best idea, but…" and she let her voice trail-off while she thought. He waited to let her think for a little, and then finally she said, "You know, Abe, I think we can do without the electric and indoor plumbing. I've never had it, and you've never had it, so what's the difference? It looks tempting, but I have no problem with not having it."

"I feel exactly the same way, but I want you to be satisfied. Most of those I have talked to, including my father, don't have a huge problem with it one way or another. They all felt it probably would be best to remove it." And he reached over and took her hand.

"The more I think about it I realize that our love and happiness do not lie in electricity or plumbing." She said seriously.

"I agree with that. Well, here we are back at the Yoder 'ranch,' we'll see what your Papa says to all this."

Joshua, Sammy, and Evangeline were always happy when Abe would stay for supper. They could sometimes entice him into a game of checkers, or caroms, or any game they thought they could beat him at.

After supper they all sat around and visited for a while and then the children were sent into the parlor so the older ones could go over the details of the farm purchase. Jacob was amazed at how much Abe had learned about real estate in just 10 days. He was, also, glad that Courtnee had given up the idea of electricity and indoor plumbing. He felt it might be a problem if some families had those "modern" things and others did not. The Emma and Brushy Prairie Churches did not believe quite so strictly as other orders of the Amish. However, they did not want to begin a "race to the world." Jacob felt that it could be possible to have electric and indoor plumbing and use them with moderation and control. They did not want to do anything that would eventually bring the world into their homes through radio and television. Jacob pondered these things. *There is no telling where something like that would stop,* he thought. *We would soon be in the world and of it too! No, I don't think we should begin it.*

After Jacob got his thoughts together he said, "Abe, you've done a good job. I would not have anything to add. Your father taught you well, and has given you sound advice."

"Well, then I'll get busy and make sure the legal work gets done." Abe was good at taking responsibility. "They said it would probably take about four weeks before we can close on the deal. Courtnee and I were thinking of setting a marriage date somewhere about two months after that. That would make it about the middle of July, is that a problem?" As he said it he turned toward Mary Emily.

After Mary Emily thought a second she said, "It couldn't be much later, the garden will be all planted and growing. Either then or October would be best for me."

"I think," Jacob chimed in, "July would be best, then you can be settled before winter. Maybe you will still have a few things to do in the house or barns."

"OK, July 18 is a Thursday in about the middle of the month, is that OK?" Abe said as he looked from one to the other. Everyone nodded. "You look a little perplexed, Honey, is this OK?"

"Oh, sure! It is getting to seems so real. It's always been kind of a dream before. July 18th is just fine."

"Shall we pray?" asked Jacob as they all bowed their heads and Jacob, praying out loud this time, asked God to bless Abe and Courtnee and their desire to set up a home that would be pleasing to Him.

*****

Several weeks later Abe took Courtnee with him to Apple Acres (Courtnee's name for their farm). He had to meet a contractor there who would be working on the house. The farm was the picture of beauty. The apple trees were all in full bloom and the bees were humming away as they worked gathering the nectar. She loved just walking between the trees and breathing in the scent of the blossoms and dreaming of what it will be like to live here — for always. Just she and Abe at first, and then maybe some little ones if the Lord should will. She wandered in and out of the house where Abe and the contractor were deep in discussion and continued dreaming. The owner said they could have all the furniture in the house, which would be a great help for them.

She could already imagine the trees hanging heavy with apples. She imagined a stand at the side of the road with bushels and bushels of glossy red fruit waiting for buyers. Forgotten were her memories of the hours and hours of work picking apples from the few trees her parents had — this orchard was over twice as big as that one! She knew, of course, that it was a dream, but she did not want it to end. *Dream on while you can, Courtnee.*

She looked at the outhouse in its sad and crumbling condition, and then thought of the nice indoor bathroom that there was in the house. It truly was inviting to just keep some of the worldly conveniences, but, *No, I've made up my mind and I'm not going to change it. I want my children to live just like I have lived.* Just then Abe and Jim, the contractor, came out of the house and shook hands, and after a few parting words Jim was gone.

"Well, how'd it go?" Courtnee asked as Abe approached her.

"Pretty good. He said he thought two thousand dollars would do it. He suggested doing the changeover in such a way that it could be reversed if we ever wanted to sell the house. The bathroom will make a nice closet."

"Sounds pretty good. How long will it take?"

"He said that he could start in about a week, and that it should take not more than two weeks. That will give us time to clean and do a little painting or wallpapering if we want."

"Did you tell him to go ahead?" Courtnee's voice was brimming with excitement.

"Yes, I did. I hope that's OK?"

"It sure is! This is all so like a dream I have to keep pinching myself to see that I am awake. It's going to be so much fun, just you and I — for a while at least. Probably a lot of work, but it will be fun work. Seeing you come clomping up on the porch with your boots, and me cooking up dinner in the kitchen. I can't wait Abe — how soon is it?"

"Just eight weeks, and we've got a lot to do. We had better go so we don't miss supper at my folks."

It only took a few minutes to get to the Schrock farm and as soon as Courtnee was in the house Cornelia was wanting on her lap. The other children, as well, all wanted to be heard at the same time. They all were so loveable. She often watched Gertrude because she wanted to be a mother just like her. Gertrude was so kind and patient and yet when she spoke — never shouting — the children knew she meant what she said. When she said, "Time for bed, kinder," that meant now, not whenever you wish. Emil was a rather quiet man, but it was evident the children all loved him and respected him. The older children liked to poke fun at him and he enjoyed it because he knew it was all in fun.

Chapter 7

As Abe slowly drove Courtnee home that evening they talked of all they needed to do in the coming weeks. It was time to really "knuckle in," as Jacob would say, and make serious plans. The wedding itself would require a lot of work. Of course, they knew they could count on the other families in Courtnee's church to help. They figured there would probably be about 100 people at the wedding.

Just then Courtnee saw a sign tacked to a telephone pole and asked, "Did you see that sign on the pole back there? I've seen several of them, but could not see what it said."

"Yes, as a matter of fact, I did see it but wasn't paying any attention to it. Shall I go back?" said Abe as he let the car slow.

"No, but let's watch and see if we see another one. I wonder what it's about. Maybe it was an auction sign." Courtnee began to think they might not see another, and was almost ready to ask Abe to turn around when they could see another sign far ahead. As they approached it Abe let the car slow and he pulled as close as he could so they could read it.

"Oh, it's just a farm sale."

"A farm sale!" Courtnee exclaimed. "That's just what we need! Does it say something about, 'north of Shipshewana'?"

"Yes, 'two miles north of Shipshewana.' You're right! It didn't dawn on me that we could get things we need there. The sale is this coming Saturday at 10:30. Let's go, shall we?"

"Yes, for sure. I'll bet our parents would like to go too. At farm sales you can usually get things at a good price. With all the furniture that is left in our house we won't need so much of that, but there are a lot of other things like kitchen stuff, and even barn stuff that we could get."

"Now that I think about it, I know just the farm. It's a large cattle operation, and that may provide some things I need as well. Let's check with our folks. But I'll pick you up about 8:00 o'clock Saturday so we can get there in time to look over what's for sale."

*****

On Saturday morning as Abe and Courtnee approached the farm, where the sale was to be held, the road was already lined with vehicles of all kinds, and on the front lawn were quite a few buggies. They certainly had not come too early!

It seemed to them the farm was already a milling sea of people, but the crowd had only begun to gather! Quite a few hayracks (the large flat wagons for hauling hay) were set out and items of every description were piled on them, and more was being brought from the various buildings including the house.

One hayrack was stacked with boxes of clothing and sewing fabric as well as piles of linen goods. Another hayrack had all sorts of kitchen utensils, and dishes, and even some soap items and other cleaners. Two more wagons were loaded with woodworking tools and garden tools and all the items used in the machine shop to maintain the tractors and other machinery. The front lawn was covered with chairs, beds, tables, and other items from the house. It was here that Courtnee spotted a treadle sewing machine, the kind that you run with your feet. This, she wanted more than anything else and she went to find Abe to see if he would bid on it for her. He was right where she thought he would be — looking over the tools.

"Abe, come here I want to show you something," she said quietly. People at auctions never want to let anyone see what they are interested in, or to call attention to something, so she pointed to the sewing machine cautiously from a distance. "That is something that I would love. Will you buy it for me and I'll pay you back?"

"Does it work?"

"Shall I try it?"

"Sure, go ahead and try it. We should know if it works. I'll buy it if you want it. Do you see anything else that you want?"

"Well, I was looking at the set of dishes on the other end of that wagon over there. They are all white and not fancy. It depends if they go for too much."

"What's too much?"

"Well, I think maybe 15 dollars. The sewing machine… maybe 25, but if it goes a little higher…"

"I know, you really want it, I'll see what I can do. You stand by and nudge me when you want me to stop."

Just then the auctioneer's voice crackled over the loud speaker, "OK, folks, gather round so we can begin this here auction." He then went over all the rules he would go by and said they would begin with the linen goods wagon, then one of the tool wagons and so on around.

Abe was buying quite a lot of tools and things and Courtnee was worried he would run out of money before the sewing machine, but she did not realize he had it all planned out. Sometimes she did not know if he was bidding or not. He had a way of catching the auctioneer's eye and then slightly raising his head — that was a bid!

It seemed no one wanted the dishes, and Abe bought them for $5.00 and Courtnee was pleased. She stood next to him with one hand on his elbow and when they held up something she wanted she gave his elbow two quick squeezes. He was thoroughly enjoying doing the bidding, and Courtnee was glad she did not have to bid.

When they got near the sewing machine Courtnee felt like her heart was going to jump right out of her chest.

Chairs and tables and beds were first and it seemed
they would never get there — and then suddenly they
were there! At first the auctioneer could not get a bid to
start it and when someone in the crowd called out
twenty-five cents the auctioneer broke out in a laugh,
"You've got to be kidding! Oh well, I'll take anything for

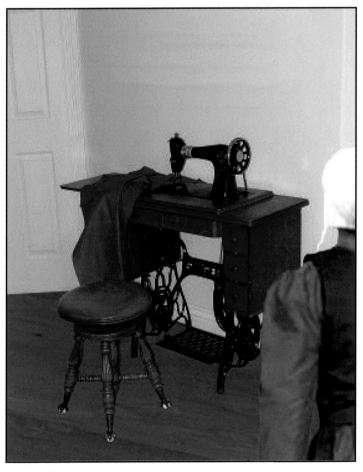

starters," and that did it. It seemed everyone wanted
the machine and Courtnee was worried. She could not
tell whether Abe was bidding or not. Well, he wasn't

bidding yet. He was waiting for things to settle down. Finally, the auctioneer got to twelve dollars and seemed to be about to close, when Abe nodded for thirteen dollars. Right away whoever else wanted it started bidding again. Now it was Abe and someone far back in the crowd she could not see. When the other bidder had the bid at eighteen dollars Abe did something that shocked everyone. He spoke out to the auctioneer and said, "Twenty-five dollars, that's my top." It so surprised the other bidder that he stopped bidding right then and there and Abe had it for twenty-five dollars, and Courtnee was thrilled!

"Great!" Abe said, "I've wanted to try that at an auction for a long time, and it worked."

As far as Courtnee was concerned the day was over. She could not wait to get the sewing machine home and try it out. It would sure beat sewing everything by hand. However, Abe had seen some tools that he wanted to get if he could so they loaded everything into Abe's truck and went back to watch the tools auctioned.

She saw several people she knew, but there was not much time to visit as long as Abe was buying, and such a deal it was! The tools were less than one-fourth the price of new ones. The sale had come at a very good time — just when they were setting up their own farm and needing almost everything — except furniture. Courtnee thought about how blessed they were to have a house with almost everything in it. She was not fussy about styles, *the Englisch can worry about that kind of thing,* she thought.

As they drove home they were both very pleased about their purchases, and they were very tired. Abe carried her machine and other purchases into her house, and declined an invitation to stay for supper. Truth be told he was ready for bed!

Chapter 8

When everyone heard that the wedding would be in the summer they were surprised, but no one complained, in fact, nearly everyone thought it was a good idea.

"I think it is a smart plan to have it in the summer for more reasons than one." Anna Mae said as she and Teena sat at the kitchen table one rainy afternoon discussing the wedding that would be in about five weeks. It did not seem to be much time to plan a wedding, "The eighteenth will roll around sooner than we think. I think we should see what Mary Emily would like us to do."

"Uh huh, sure… they would like the help… doesn't everyone… usually pitch in at weddings?" Teena said hesitantly as she looked out the window rather dreamily — something else was on her mind.

"Why do you say it like that? Don't you want to help?"

"No, but I am wondering… Oh, I guess it wouldn't work anyhow." Teena sounded rather put off or something.

"Well, go ahead and say it. You sound awful down. I didn't think this wedding was bothering you, with you and Everett and all."

"Well, no it isn't," Teena had an idea, which she really wanted to do, but felt it would be too much for her mother. "I'll tell you what I'm thinking. I really would like to have a surprise kitchen party for both Courtnee and Sandy — you know, one where everybody brings some kind of food? But it may be too much for you."

"No, no, no! That would really be fun. Great idea! Oh, I think that would be great fun. Let's see… next Sunday is church Sunday, but we could do it on the following one."

"Oh, I didn't think you would like the idea. We will have to somehow let everyone know <u>except</u> the four. We could hide all the cars and have everyone in the house when they arrive. Let's not even tell the one couple that the other is coming. Shall it be after supper?"

Soon Teena and her mother had it all planned out and the preparations began. Baking and cleaning… baking and cleaning… it seemed like that was all they did. They had decided the party would be after supper so they would not have to make a meal. Even Menno got into it by cleaning up the barn and barn lot. When the day arrived everything was in readiness. Menno had even prepared a place behind some trees in a pasture where the cars and the MacDonald's buggy could be parked. Abe's whole family came, as did Everett's. Sandy's parents were there. Even the Miller's came from Nappanee, and Courtnee's grandma Beiler. Teena never got a final count but she reckoned there were about 55 present.

The surprise worked just fine. Everyone sat quietly when John and Sandy's car drove in followed almost immediately by Abe and Courtnee. Evangeline was peaking out the kitchen window and reporting what was happening outside. They all got out and were very surprised to see each other, but did not detect anything unusual. Then when they walked into the house everyone shouted, "SURPRISE!" Teena thought Sandy

---

Pickled Crab Apples

3 lb Crab Apples	1 cup Water
2 lb Sugar	¼ cup Stick Cinnamon
½ cup Vinegar	2 tbsp Whole Cloves

Wash the crab apples but do not remove the stems. Have ready a syrup made by boiling sugar, vinegar, and water for 10 minutes; add spices, then add a few crab apples with 1 or 2 cloves pressed into each. Let it cook until softened. Put apples into sterilized jars. When all are cooked, reduce the syrup and with it fill the jars to overflowing and seal.

---

and Courtnee were going to faint, but they soon recovered and joined in the fun — and what fun it was!

Everyone had brought two food items, but the gifts were not wrapped and there were no names of who brought which, it was a gift from everyone. Anna Mae and Teena had set up a table at one end of the kitchen and it was stacked high with all manner of canned goods including; flour, sugar, salt, and there were even two smoked hams. It would be for Courtnee and Sandy to divide the items up, but that would not be a problem, the girls were good at sharing, and there were two of each of most items.

Sandy spoke first saying, "It is so sweet of you all to do this. I hardly know how to say thank you. John and I will think of this happy surprise for many years to come. Thank you!"

"I feel just like Sandy," Courtnee beamed a smile to everyone, "This is so practical, because it won't be long and we will certainly be glad we have all this. Thank you very much from Abe and I." She reached and took Abe by the arm.

It seemed everyone started talking at once. They were wishing the two couples a happy marriage — even though Sandy and John were not to be married for several months. It seemed that both couples had the respect and admiration of everyone, which is very important when entering into marriage. Courtnee and Abe had often talked about how they wanted to be sure everyone was happy about their intention to marry — especially their parents.

"Could I have everyone's attention," Menno had to shout to be heard. And then when the clamor had quieted, "Thank you. We would like to have a word of prayer and then sing some hymns. I think it would be good to pray aloud this time. If everyone would bow their heads I will pray." So he prayed and asked the Lord to bless the young couples and the other young ones who may be thinking of marriage. He asked Him to bless all who attended this gathering. And he ended,

"In the precious name of the Lord Jesus, we ask this. Amen."

Evangeline immediately turned to her mother and whispered to her mother, "Why did he ask his prayer in Jesus' Name?"

"The Scripture says something like 'Whatever you do, do it in the name of Jesus Christ.' All your prayers, in fact, everything we do should be done in His name." Whispered Mary Emily.

"I never knew that; I guess I never noticed anyone say it before."

"Well, God knew that you did not know so I am sure He accepted your prayers. But now that you know it you should do it." Her mother was always so gracious, but meanwhile the preparations for the singing were being made.

Matthew MacDonald was selected, as he often was, to start the tunes. The young people liked many of the tunes he started because they were a bit livelier. The evening was a happy and joyous time and it passed all too swiftly. Because they had started after supper it made the evening a little shorter and soon everyone began to excuse themselves with each giving one last blessing upon the couples. All too soon it was just Courtnee and Abe, and Sandy and John with Teena's family.

"Teena, you and your folks have made this a wonderful evening, thank you… so much," Sandy said as she gave Teena a big hug.

Courtnee just hugged Teena. Tears were streaming down her cheeks, and she couldn't speak, words just would not come. Teena too was weeping, and then soon Sandy was wiping her eyes. But they had to dry away the tears and begin dividing the food gifts.

Menno had thought ahead and got some empty cardboard cartons from the grocery store, which helped immensely to take the gifts home. Soon each car was loaded with boxes and the two couples were on their way home. John had a long way to go to take Sandy all the way to Goshen and then return to his home, but he did not mind.

Although she was tired, Teena sat in the kitchen with her father and mother for a long time recounting the whole evening. It was full of happy memories for them as well, and even Everett had been there and readily joined in the fun and the singing. Teena was so pleased!

*****

The next morning Courtnee awoke and as she was dressing the thought suddenly struck her that it was now less than four weeks to her wedding. As she entered the kitchen her mother was already preparing breakfast. "Mamma, it's only 26 days to my wedding. How are we going to get everything done." She wailed.

"Oh, don't worry, sweetie, we'll get it done. We are not planning something fancy like I hear the Englisch do. Anna Mae spoke to me last night and said she and Teena want to help, so I'm going to plan a day pretty soon."

"It's sooo nice of them! Teena has been just like a sister."

"She sure has. How is the repair on your house going?"

"It's going just fine. I think Jim will be done this week some time, and then we will do some painting and wallpapering — so I think that is working out just fine. Abe has been cleaning and working on the barn, and I think he has the outhouse in working order again. When Abe plans something he sticks with it until it's done."

"Well, I guess you've done your share of painting and wallpapering around here so you'll surely know how to do it. Do you remember how you used to moan about it?"

"Yeah, but it's different when it's your own place!"

So when the day came that Abe told Courtnee it was their turn to work on the house she was ready — well, as ready as she ever could be at this late date. She was certainly not fussy about the colors of the walls, nor the wallpaper and it did not take long to buy the supplies. Abe said they would have to plan to work for two days and then he would have to work with the cattle and help his father for two days. It was a good thing because Courtnee found the work very tiring and was glad to have two days to be at home and help there.

"I'll bet you never noticed," her mother said one day, "I planted a lot of celery in the spring. I just thought that we might have a wedding soon and this way we would be ready."

"Why celery?"

"Actually I don't know! It's some kind of ancient tradition for all our weddings. It was probably rather silly of me, but I did think it would be nice."

"That is so nice of you Mamma, you think of everything. I suppose I could get married without it, but it will be nice."

"Well," her mother said laughing, "you will have to get married without it because something ate off all the young plants." Then they both laughed until their sides were sore. This was going to be a very happy wedding, indeed!

Chapter 9

As the wedding day approached the repairs and redecorating was coming along very nicely, as well as the preparations at Courtnee's home where the wedding would be held. On several days Evie came along to Apple Acres with Courtnee and she was a great help. She cleaned while Courtnee helped Abe wallpaper. Wallpapering works much better if there are two people. When Evie finished with the kitchen it fairly sparkled and Courtnee was very pleased.

When Abe and Courtnee finished a room whatever furniture they had was set in it, and soon the whole house was quite livable. *It is going to be so nice to come home from the wedding to our very own place,* Courtnee thought.

Anna Mae and Teena had spent several days helping Mary Emily with all the preparations. The house was cleaned from top to bottom. The cakes and cookies were baked and stored away, and when that last Wednesday arrived, the day before the wedding, everything was ready. The Yoder farm had never been so clean and orderly. The meeting room was also ready because several of the interior walls were moveable so nearly the whole first floor was one big room. They thought it would accommodate everyone for the 'meeting' but for the meal they would have to eat in shifts.

*****

As everyone gathered on that Tuesday morning it became evident to Jacob that they were going to have an overflow crowd. He went into the meeting room/ parlor and asked everyone to sit as closely together as possible, but even then many stood in the kitchen until it was full and then some of the men stood outside by the opened windows in order to hear.

Courtnee was dressed in her beautiful new deep emerald green dress and white apron, which she had sewn on her 'new' machine. Her new head covering set off her radiant face perfectly as she was smiling almost continuously. Her rosy colored cheeks gave her just the color she needed to be a beautiful bride.

Abe was dressed traditionally in a new long sleeved white shirt and new black trousers with the usual black suspenders. His face was the picture of calmness and readiness to proceed. He looked very pleased!

As they sat in the front row facing the preachers the little girls took turns sneaking up along the seats to take a peak at Courtnee. She was the model of everything they dreamed of. Soon the crowd was packed into the room so tightly that the little girls could no longer sneak up to see Courtnee, they would have to wait until later, and, anyway, it was time for the first hymn to be sung.

Courtnee thought she had never listened to any sermon so intently. The preacher spoke about the marriage

bond and how pleasing it was to God. He spoke about
how they should be faithful to each other and to God,
and that Jesus should have a place in their home, "and
not just a pretty plaque on the wall." He then went on
to speak about the place the man and woman should
have in the marriage; that the man was to be the head
just as Christ is Head of the Church; and how the
woman was to look to her husband for everything, and
that as under his headship she was to rule the house.
He ended up speaking about how the whole marriage
bond was to reflect the relationship of Christ to His
Church, and how He, that is, Christ, loves His Bride,
the Church. Every word sank deeply into Courtnee's
heart and she wanted to do everything just as he said.

Then followed the actual marriage ceremony and
Courtnee found herself trembling a little and when she
joined hands with Abe he noticed it and gave her hand
several little squeezes as if to say "everything will be
alright." Then the final hymn was given out and Mr.
Miller gave the final prayer and the service was over —
so she thought; it was then that she heard a voice in the
back of the room asking to sing another hymn… and it
was her favorite! She then recognized the voice was
that of Menno. It was very unusual for him to do that,
but… *it is just like him,* she thought, *he knows that is
my favorite.* Everyone sang if very lustily.

It was not until then that she noticed how hot the room
was. Abe's shirt was soaked with perspiration — and
then she noticed everyone was dripping with sweat.
Suddenly she felt she needed to get outside.

"Abe, can we go outside right away. I am so hot I think I'll faint," she whispered.

"I feel the same. Follow close behind me and don't talk to anyone."

Although it was "July warm" outside she felt so much better. They were immediately surrounded by the young and old alike wishing them well, and she noticed quite a few of the little ones just standing and looking and she supposed they were wondering what this was all about. One after another of her friends came up and she regretted that she did not have more time to talk to them; she could just hug them and say a few words, making a mental note to invite them over soon for a visit.

For the wedding meal they were seated in the traditional manner at the corner table, but the others

---

Taffy Apples

6 - 8 Apples
2 cups Brown Sugar
½ cup water

½ tsp White Karo syrup
½ tsp Lemon extract

Choose firm, ripe apples and put a stick four inches long in each one — insert it at the stem or flower end. Boil sugar, water, and syrup together until a little dropped into cold water forms a hard ball, or to 310° (if you have a thermometer). Remove from the fire, add lemon extract and dip apples into the syrup mixture until they are covered. Set them on a buttered plate to cool.

had to eat in several shifts. Courtnee was very conscious of being the center of attention, a thing she was not used to and did not like, and it caused her cheeks to feel hot! *Now I know why that bride I once saw looked like she used make-up, she was probably hot too. I probably look that way myself!* When she looked over at Abe he looked the same, except he was just plain hot. Sweat was beaded on his forehead and his shirt was soaked. Although he was smiling and speaking very calmly to everyone she could tell he was miserable inside. *When will this be over? It is so nice of everyone to come and join in, but I am tired and want to go home. Home! That's it, our very own home.*

"Courtnee, dear, you look so tired." It was her mother's voice that broke through her thoughts.

"I am. I am hot and tired, and my face is even sore from smiling. When will this be over, Mamma?"

"This is the last group to be served, then you are free to go. Abe looks as tired as you. It has been a long, but a very good day. Everyone seems so happy with your marriage; it's as if God sent His blessing too.

"I don't think I have ever talked so much and listened so much," Abe interjected.

"I think as soon as these folks are finished, or nearly finished, you could excuse yourselves, I don't think it would hurt a bit," said Mary Emily.

"Thanks!" Both of them spoke at once and then looked at each other with a tired and tender smile.

When they walked into the house at Apple Acres, a short while later, everything seemed so different. They had been in there many times, even worked in the house, but it was all different now. This time they were man and wife. Abe took Courtnee in his arms for the first time in a tender hug and kissed her with a long, lingering kiss.

"Ah! Our first kiss! That was super!" he whispered.

Courtnee just reached for another. "Mmmmm!" was all she could say. *I'll never forget this as long as I live,* she thought.

Chapter 10

The next morning the birds had been singing for a long time and the sun was high in the sky before either of them stirred. They had been thoroughly exhausted from the day before, their wedding day.

"Good morning, Mrs. Schrock!" Courtnee heard a voice say just as she was becoming conscious of where she was.

"Oh!" She exclaimed, "isn't this wonderful, Abe." She stretched, yawned, and continued, "simply wonderful. Just us…" but she could say no more as Abe had reached over and was hugging her.

"You know, sweetheart, you are a mess in the morning. Your hair is a mess," he said as he tousled her hair.

"Well, you aren't so cute in the morning yourself!" She shot back as she gave him a jab in the ribs and they had a fit of laughter together.

"Let's have some breakfast, what do you say?" Abe said as he bounded out of bed.

"Great, what are you making?"

"Me? Didn't I tell you I can't even boil water? Remember, the wife is supposed to do everything the husband wants." He said with an impish grin as he deliberately misquoted the preacher.

"The preacher also said, 'husbands love your wife' and I think the preacher said something like you wouldn't ask your wife to do something you wouldn't do." She could hardly get the words out for laughing.

As she stood up he took her in his arms and hugged her again. "You know something?" he asked. "I think Mr. Schrock just got an armful of a very sweet something that's more than he can handle!"

*****

They sat for a long time at breakfast, or was it lunch? They were savoring every feature of their first day of married life and did not care what time it was. It was really fun to smell the new paint mixed with all the other odors of the old house. From the kitchen table they could see several trees of the orchard and a corner of the barn — their orchard and their barn!

"Let's go out and explore around, Abe."

"That's a good idea. When I was working over here I was so busy I didn't take even one minute to look around."

They bounded through the door like two children and nearly ran smack dab into Teena and Everett who were just tip-toeing up the steps. Neither Courtnee nor Abe had heard them drive up and it was no wonder, because they had parked way out near the road and quietly walked up hoping to surprise them, and they did.

After talking and laughing for a bit, they all joined together to go exploring. Teena was as excited as if the farm were hers. The apple trees were already loaded with apples — green apples, sour apples. They found an old garden plot, but it was so full of weeds they hardly recognized it.

"I think if I plow it up it should be just about the right size, don't you think?" Abe said turning to Courtnee.

"We might not need all of it, Abe. Mamma's garden was about this big, but she was feeding all of us."

"Yeah, you're right."

"Are you going to have a roadside stand?" Everett seemed to have an eye for business, "You've got the perfect place for one out there where we parked, and this road is pretty busy. I think you would do real good."

"Funny you should ask that. Courtnee said the same thing the first time she saw the place. I haven't counted the fruit trees, but I'll bet there are maybe twelve or so, and I think there are a couple of other kinds of fruit, but I'm not sure which kind. See that tree over there? Its bark is different than the apple trees."

"That's a pear tree, and the one next to it is a peach," Everett seemed quite knowledgeable on fruit trees. "I like all kinds of plants, but especially trees. I have a little book and have studied it quite a lot. See that tree over kinda' close to the barn, it's a cherry — a sour cherry, but they make good pies!"

"Well, it sure looks like we've got something going here. We are not sure what we want to do yet. I've got to bring my herd of cattle over soon. I want to keep a close eye on all the calves. I think Courtnee would like to have some chickens — I don't know about any other poultry, but we'll see. She has always liked sheep, and we've got one pasture where sheep might do pretty good."

"You know, Abe, I was just noticing that stand of trees back there," he pointed beyond the barn, " we might do some pretty decent deer hunting there. That's on your property isn't it?"

"No. It's on the neighbor's land. But all is not lost because I know him and I think he will let us in at deer hunting season."

"Well, I hate to break this up," Everett said as he turned to see where the girls had gone. "I think we had better be going. We'll have to find the girls."

It did not take long to find them. They had set down in the midst of the apple trees and were having a good visit. They both moaned when Everett announced they would need to leave. He had a pile of farm work waiting for him since he had let most of it go to be at the wedding. Courtnee and Abe stood arm in arm waving until Everett's car was out of sight.

Chapter 11

"Hello, m'love," Abe said as he came in for lunch several days later, "That sounds quite Englisch, doesn't it! Yum, something sure smells good." He said as he put his arm around her and stole a quick kiss.

"I hope it tastes as good," and she gave him one of her million dollar smiles.

"Well, I plowed and disked the garden, but it is going to take a lot of work to get it ready to plant. I think it is too late to plant anything this year, but whatever we do now will help for next spring."

"I'll work on it whenever I get some time and try to get the weeds and grass raked out." Then after a moment of silence she said, "Abe how about inviting your whole family over for supper on this Lord's Day. It is not a meeting day is it?"

"No, it is not a meeting day. Do you think we could fit them in?"

"I think we could if we squeeze in and use the folding table in the parlor for some of the younger ones. If you think it is a good idea why don't you invite them next time you go to help your Papa?"

Of course, Emil and Gertrude were quite pleased and agreed to come. The little children were overjoyed when they heard of it, and Courtnee set to work making plans and even preparing some baked goods. Suddenly it struck her that they did not have enough chairs — table space was not a big problem, but chairs were.

"Abe, we've got one problem that I had not thought about — chairs. What can we do?" She whined.

"Let's count how many we need and I'll ask the folks to bring some."

"Good!"

When the day came and whole Schrock family came trooping in, most of them carrying a chair. It looked so funny Courtnee got the giggles and could hardly get the meal together for thinking about this whole line of people coming in each with a chair. "It reminds me of what Jesus said to the lame man, 'pick thy couch and walk,'" she told Gertrude who was giggling right along with Courtnee.

"Just never you mind, ve are only so pleased to come, jah?" Gertrude said as she handed Courtnee a basket with a large slab of smoked bacon and some jellies.

"Oh, thank you so much — may I call you Mamma?"

"Och, I vould be ever so pleased. You are my favorite daughter-in-law, you know."

"I am so blessed to be a part of Abe's family. We are going to be so happy together."

"Jah, I know vhat you mean, but difficult times vill surely come, and you must work as hard or harder at staying close to the Lord. Be sure, Dear, to help Abe to remember to have your daily devotions, I mean read the Word, and pray, and meditate. It is so easy to get involved with your home life and farm that you forget — I know, because there vas a time in our marriage vhen ve totally forgot the Lord, except to go through the motions of going to Church, and such."

"Thank you, Mamma." Courtnee whispered as a tear rolled down her cheek. She threw her arms about Gertrude and held her tight. Gertrude was pleased because Courtnee was so moved by what she had said. It then took Courtnee a few seconds to come "down to earth" as they say, and get on with the meal, but she kept Gertrude's words of advice in her heart. She wanted to have a good long chat with her some day. This thought, too, was submerged in the busy-ness of the moment.

The Schrock family visit went very well, although Courtnee was quite nervous that the meal might not all get done and ready to eat at the same time — but it was! Everyone was so busy chatting and laughing that even if something did not turn out right they never would have noticed. Abe's sister Grace was an excellent help in the kitchen and even Anja helped clear off the table after the meal and Gertrude washed up.

Suddenly the evening was over and Courtnee sank into the sofa and breathed a deep sigh. "You did a wonderful job, Sweetheart." Abe said as he snuggled up close, "That was truly amazing how you got that all together in a new kitchen and all!"

"Boy was I worried that I would forget something, or that the corn wouldn't be done on time or something. It always seemed so easy for Mamma, but I guess that is what you call experience." She giggled and said, "I'm not giving up Abe. I'm going to master it, you give me the confidence."

"OK, then when are we going to have your family over, and then Menno's, and…" She held up her hand to stop him.

"Let's get some sleep now, and talk about it later — I'm tired to the bone."

Abe said nothing but gathered her into his arms and held her close.

*****

It was only several days later that Abe announced that he was going the next morning to help his father for three or four hours and his mother wondered if Courtnee would like to visit and stay for lunch. He did not have to ask twice, Courtnee was pleased with the invitation. *Maybe we can continue the visit Gertrude started when she came for supper*, Courtnee wondered.

When they arrived Gertrude was making several pies. She was planning to send two pies to an Englisch neighbor who had recently lost a baby and she thought it might cheer them up.

"Och! That must be hard… awful hard to lose a little one like that, but ve must go on living ve cannot give up, jah?"

"We just read the Scripture this morning, 'I can do all through Christ which strengtheneth me,' in Philippians 4. It takes on a whole new meaning when I think it could have been Abe and I."

"I am glad to hear that you are reading the Word in the mornings, and praying, too, I hope?"

"Oh, yes. Abe said he always wants to start each day like that and I am in favor of it too."

"Gut, Gut! You know, I have said a few tings about your marriage to Abe, because Emil and I love you both very much and do not vant anyting to come between you. I think it is best to say these tings early — before they happen. Do you know vhat I mean?"

"I am glad for your help, Mamma. Abe will be too, I am sure."

"Too many marriages go sour! It is terrible to hear about husbands and wives who do not get along much less get divorced. Even among us, you know. One of the most important tings in a marriage is communications — talk everyting over. Even if you don't agree with your partner — and it vill happen — talk, talk, talk. Abe is a very go-ahead boy, he is a good boy, but he vants to get tings done. Maybe sometimes for you too fast ! Oh, I don't vant to say too much, but I vant to encourage you to talk with him — and I've told him the same."

Courtnee was nodding her head in agreement all the time Gertrude talked. "Go ahead, Mamma, I hope I can just remember what you have said."

"Vell, I have this letter, it is a very old letter, an old lady wrote it to Emil and I ven ve vere first married. She vas an old family friend, but she vas very close to the Savior and she wrote it. I vould like if you vould take and copy it, and then really read it. Emil and I read it over many times in those early years. Ve had some big disappointments and got very out of sorts vit God, but He brought us back to Him — praise His Name!"

"Oh, I'd very much appreciate it if I could copy it, it will mean a lot to me because it came from you, even if you didn't write it."

"I vill haf to look for it and then I'll give it to you."

As they finished talking the pies were done and it was time to begin cooking lunch, but Courtnee was very pleased for her mother-in-law's advice and she was looking forward to see the letter.

Living with Abe was as good and even better than she had expected. There were lots of things ahead of them. Some of them not so very good, and some of them wonderful good! They were both anxious to have some little ones playing on the parlor floor, but closer at hand was the apple harvest. If the apples were as good as they looked right now they were going to have many bushels — *maybe Everett is right, we should set up a stand at the road.*

The End

My Dear Girl Gertrude,

As your marriage day draws near my thoughts go to you
with affection, and I should like to send a few lines
that might perhaps be of help in days to come.

You are going to merge your life with another, to
become one. This is God's great institution; and while
the world has made it unholy, in His eyes it is still holy
as taken up with Him. "Marriage is honorable in all, and
the bed undefiled." (Heb. 13:4) You are, according to
His thought, to be one in heart and mind and body.

This does not, however, mean uncontrolled indulgence.
We are not to go to excess in anything that is natural,
whether eating, or drinking, or in these other matters.
Part of the fruit of the Spirit is self-control — you can
help your husband in this, as he will doubtless help you
— it is a matter of living in piety, in the fear of God.

I am writing very plainly, dear Gertrude, because I
want you to be happy. I spoke of oneness, too, in heart
and mind. But this will not come about automatically —
you have to bring it about. This is another point where
so many get tripped up. It is bound to be that some
differences will arise, no matter how much you love
each other. This is especially so in the first year when
you are getting adjusted to each other. But the
adjustment period can be made much, much easier by
wisdom and unselfishness. Study each other, learn to
know the little peculiarities and tastes of each other
and consider for them. Do not press your own likes and
dislikes; let each be ready to yield a point to the
other. "The wisdom from above is... gentle, and easy to

be entreated," (Jas 3:17) is a wonderful motto for new husbands and wives.

Of course, I have not spoken of headship in all the foregoing. I think, dear girl, that you are quite clear about it. One sure way to misery in marriage is to disregard headship. Whether the husband or the wife is the stronger character has nothing to do with it. If the husband does not take on headship, the godly wife will give it to him. Headship does not mean giving orders; it works by influence and guidance as the sun does in the solar system. The true husband and wife consult together and pray together about everything. But final decisions and general directions of matters come from the head (the husband) by getting wisdom from his Head – Christ. It may seem at times that the husband's decision is a mistake. But let the godly wife submit, and pray. Then God will either show the husband that he is wrong, and he will change; or God will show the wife that, after all, she was mistaken. The wife who accepts headship with God will generally have no complaints. As to the "nourishing and cherishing," which is the husband's side, he will give it devotedly to such a wife if he is with God.

In the ups and downs, the little differences that arise, do not air each other's weaknesses outside. Keep all the troubles shut within the four walls, and they will evaporate much faster. Times may come when the husband or wife may need to seek the comments and advice of a godly brother or sister, then such may be of great value.

2

I have spoken, dear Gertrude, of your being one, but that is in your earthly setting only; you will not, as you know, be one in heaven. So hold firmly and constantly to your own individual life with God. Read and meditate and pray alone as well as with your husband. Gain spiritual substance for yourself, that you may be a true helpmate to him, and have something for the service of God.

Do not forget both the morning and the evening "lamb" together — in the morning minutes may be few, but five minutes together householdly and a verse or two and prayer, is a right start and honoring to God. There may be time for a little longer devotion in the evening.

Well, dear Gertrude, my pen has run along at great length. May God bless this union very, very much, dear girl, and may the Lord Jesus and His people find rest and refreshment in your home.

With much warm love,

Your sister in Him
　　Mary

ACKNOWLEDGMENTS

It is with great pleasure that I now present this book, and wish to acknowledge the help I have received in making Courtnee's story possible. Without my granddaughters Alanna, Vivian, and Elaine who posed for some of my pictures my job would have been very difficult and I may have given up. Don Croskey, of Killbuck, Ohio has been very helpful in supplying many of the background photos for all my "Courtnee" books. I could not have had so many photos without his kind assistance. Also, I wish to thank Karen Town (photographer) and her daughter Kassidy for the "grown up" photos of Courtnee. Although they live in England they have been very kind and cooperative.

Then last but not least I wish to extend my love and thanks to my wife, Doris, who has put up with endless 'talk' about our 'eleventh' grandchild, "Courtnee." She goes with me on endless trips in my research and has read and re-read my manuscripts. She, also, has checked all the recipes, and she made the quilt in the Sandy book — a very difficult task. She made all the dresses and prayer caps for my models — and it was all just for me! To say the least she has been my best supporter and encourager!

My thanks to all of you who have given me the needed encouragement with your letters and eMail.

B. Kjellberg

October 2006

The Farm Girl Series Books

This series of stories is about a Plain farm girl named Courtnee Anne Yoder who lives with her family among the Amish. Her story begins in Northern Indiana when she is 10 years old and continues until she is married. She learns many Christian lessons and moral values. She has many friends and some interesting experiences, especially when the new teacher arrives, or when she meets Sandy - a city girl.

The author takes the reader on a journey that is fun as well as wholesome. Along side of some pointers of how a Christian young person should live are fun projects like Courtnee's quilt, and many recipes. Each book is about 90 pages long, 5.5" X 8.5" with many color photos.

$ **7.95** each + $ 2.50 shipping ($ 5.00 for all 4 books)

Personal Checks

KJELLBERG PUBLISHING

Voice Mail: 630-653-6419
P.O.Box 725 Wheaton, IL 60187 USA
eMail: wsc@kjellbergprinting.com

Money Orders

Generous Dealer Discounts Available

ABOUT THE AUTHOR

The author was born on a farm west of Chicago, Illinois. He is the father of three grown children who now have their own families. Printing and publishing has provided a living. His closeness to books and publishing over the years has created a desire to fulfill a lifelong dream, that of writing. Seeing a need for children to have solid basic Christian teaching motivated him to launch into authoring.

He still lives in the area and has been closely in touch with farming all his life. This proximity to areas where the Amish live has given him easy access to observe and learn their ways. (*See the comments about his purpose on page 5.*) He has long been interested in them as a people and admires their readiness to live, as they believe. Many hours have been spent soaking up their lifestyle.

It was a porcelain doll that the author sculpted and made that inspired the story of Courtnee Anne Yoder. Her life is like many other farm girl's lives - not filled with suspense, but a lot of fun and simple experiences.

One of the objectives of the author is to encourage a wholesome Christian lifestyle based on the Bible. Aware of the "slide" in morals in the world in general, he feels children and young people need to be encouraged, even taught, what the real standard is - God's Word, and he hopes this story will do just this.